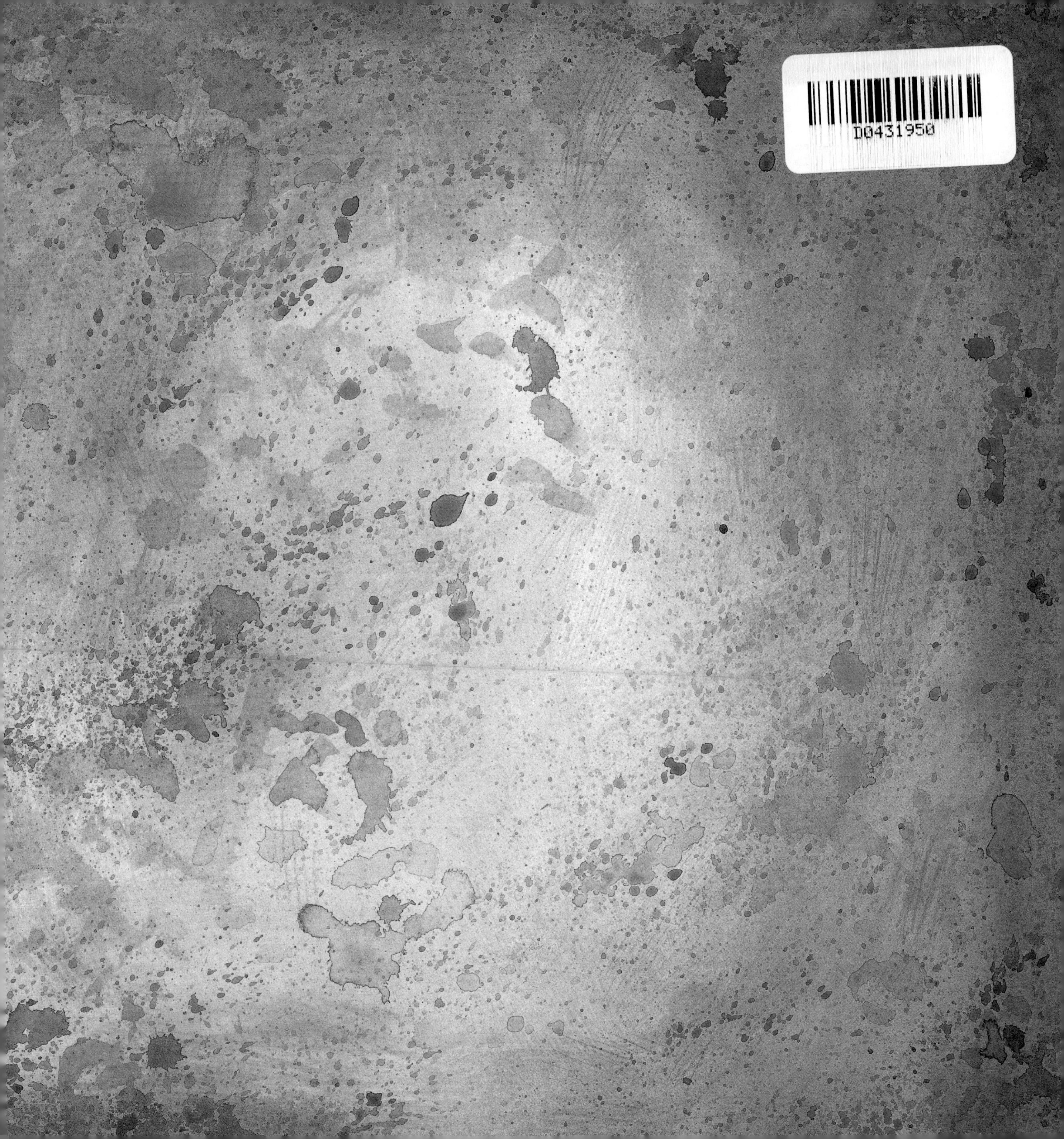
D0431950

Together
Always

FOR ALEX & HENRY
—EW

ALLA MIA
AMICA TIZIANA
—LM

STERLING CHILDREN'S BOOKS
New York

An Imprint of Sterling Publishing Co., Inc.
1166 Avenue of the Americas
New York, NY 10036

First Sterling edition published in 2017.

ISBN 978-1-4549-2326-8

Distributed in Canada by Sterling Publishing
c/o Canadian Manda Group, 664 Annette Street
Toronto, Ontario, Canada M6S 2C8

For information about custom editions, special sales, and premium and corporate purchases, please contact
Sterling Special Sales at 800-805-5489 or specialsales@sterlingpublishing.com.

Manufactured in China

Lot #:
2 4 6 8 10 9 7 5 3 1
11/16

www.sterlingpublishing.com

Designed by Hannah Janzen

Together Always

BY EDWINA WYATT

ILLUSTRATED BY LUCIA MASCIULLO

STERLING CHILDREN'S BOOKS
New York

From time to time, there were cherries
and plums in the orchard.
From time to time, there were apples
and pears.

But no matter what hung from the trees,
Pig and Goat were always together.

Side by side.

When Pig got lost, Goat found the way.

When Goat felt blue, Pig told a story.

“We will stick together,” said Goat.

“Always?”

“Always.”

So Pig and Goat stuck together in the orchard.
Together in the sun.
Together in the stream.

Days were lazy.
Days were long.

When Pig felt small, Goat told tall tales.

When Goat couldn't sleep, Pig would hum.

“We will stick together,” said Goat.

“Always?”

“Always.”

So Pig and Goat stuck together in the orchard.

Together in the peace.
Together in the quiet.

Nights were cozy.
Nights were calm.

One night, when the moon was round, Goat felt BIG!
“Let’s go!” cried Goat at the gate. “I want to go everywhere!
I want to do everything!”

“But I do not,” whispered Pig.

“But we must stick together,” cried Goat.

“Always?”

“Always.”

So Pig and Goat stuck together.
Together through the gate.
Together through the mist.

Together over roots.
Together over rocks.

Climbing higher
and higher.

But Pig longed
for the orchard.

“Let’s go home,” said Pig.
“I miss the trees and the stream.”

“But I do not!” sang Goat.
“I like the wind and the rocks.”

“Then I will go home alone,” said Pig.

“But we should stick together!”
cried Goat. “*Always!*”

GOODBYE,
GOAT.

GOODBYE,
PIG.

Alone over rocks, alone over roots, Pig got lost.

But he looked this way and that, just like Goat, and found the way.

In the gray mist, in the shadows and trees, Pig felt small.

But he told tall tales, just like Goat, until he reached the gate.

Alone on the ridge, alone in the wind, Goat felt blue.
So he told a story, just like Pig, and felt better.

High on the hill, filled with new smells and sounds,
Goat couldn't sleep.

So he hummed a tune, just like Pig, until he nodded off.

In the orchard, there were sweet new cherries and plums.

Pig snuffled in the sun.
Snuffled in the stream.

Days were lazy. Days were long.

Pig saw rocks on the bank and remembered Goat.
He saw clouds in the sky and remembered Goat.

On the hill, there were sweet new mushrooms and blackberries.
Goat leaped on the rocks. Leaped on the ridge.

Nights were windy.
Nights were wild!

Goat saw moss in the grass and remembered Pig.
He saw stars in the sky and remembered Pig.

When the moon rose over the orchard,
Pig said, “Goodnight, Goat.”

And when the moon rose over the hill,
Goat said, “Goodnight, Pig.”

Sometimes Pig wondered what Goat was doing, high on the hill.

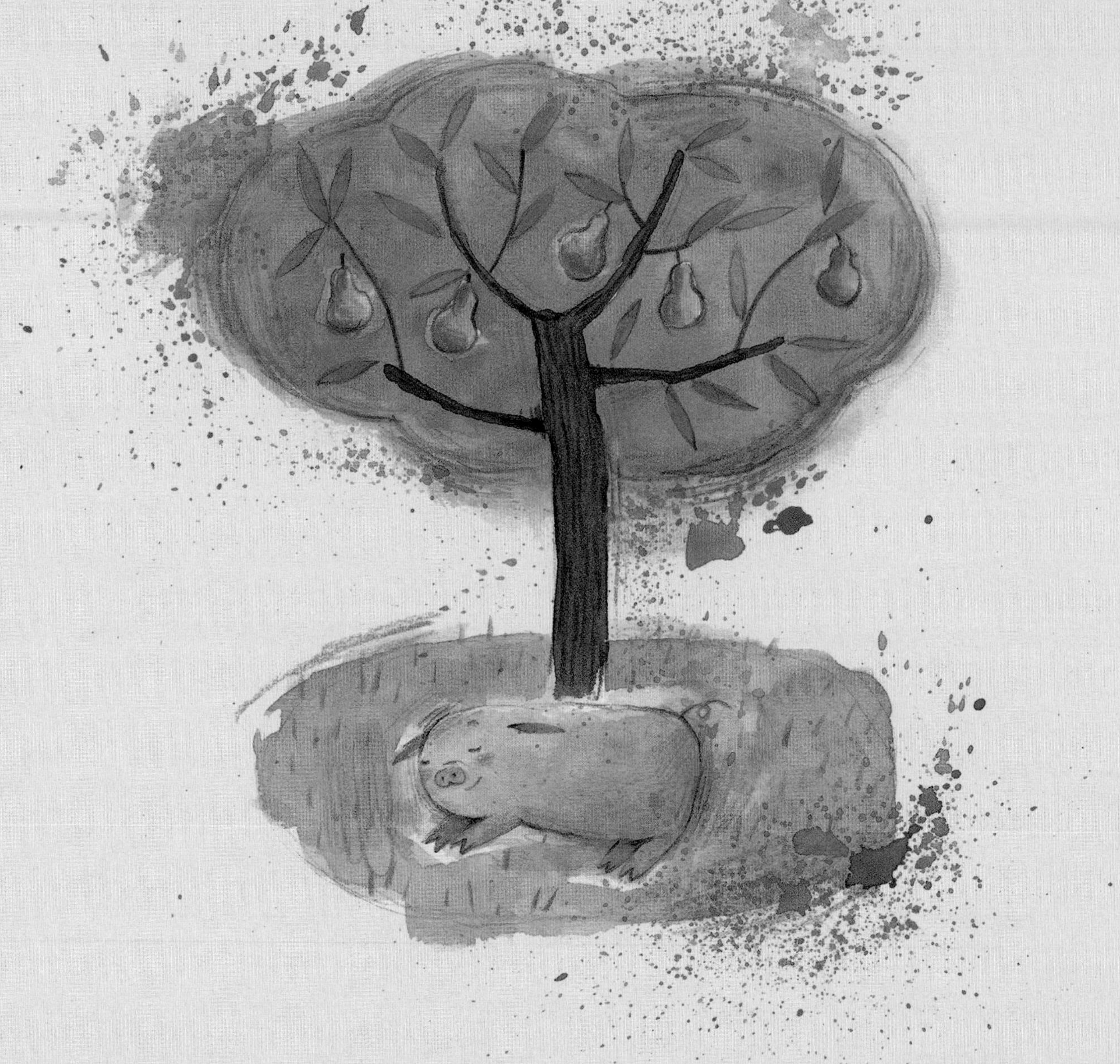

Pig wondered if Goat ever thought about dozing under pear trees.
About spotting fish in the stream.

Sometimes Goat wondered what Pig was doing, down in the orchard.

Goat wondered if Pig ever thought about leaping through wildflowers.
About finding caves in the rocks.

When the first leaves fell to the ground,
Pig saw something by the gate.

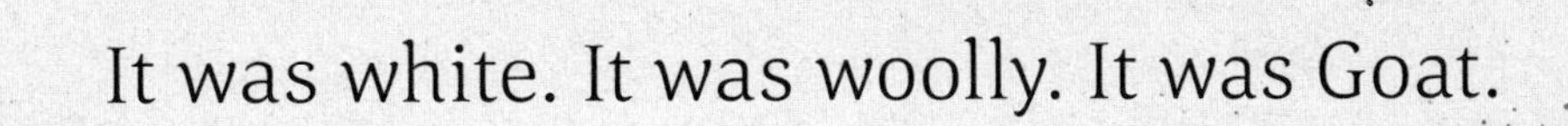

It was white. It was woolly. It was Goat.

“I missed you, Goat,” said Pig.

“I missed you, too, Pig,” said Goat.

“But you were with me,” said Pig. “Always!”

“We were together,” said Goat. “*Always.*”

From time to time, Pig snuffled alone in the orchard.

From time to time, Goat leaped alone on the hill.

But no matter what hung from the trees,
Pig and Goat were *always* together.

GOODNIGHT,
PIG.

GOODNIGHT,
GOAT.

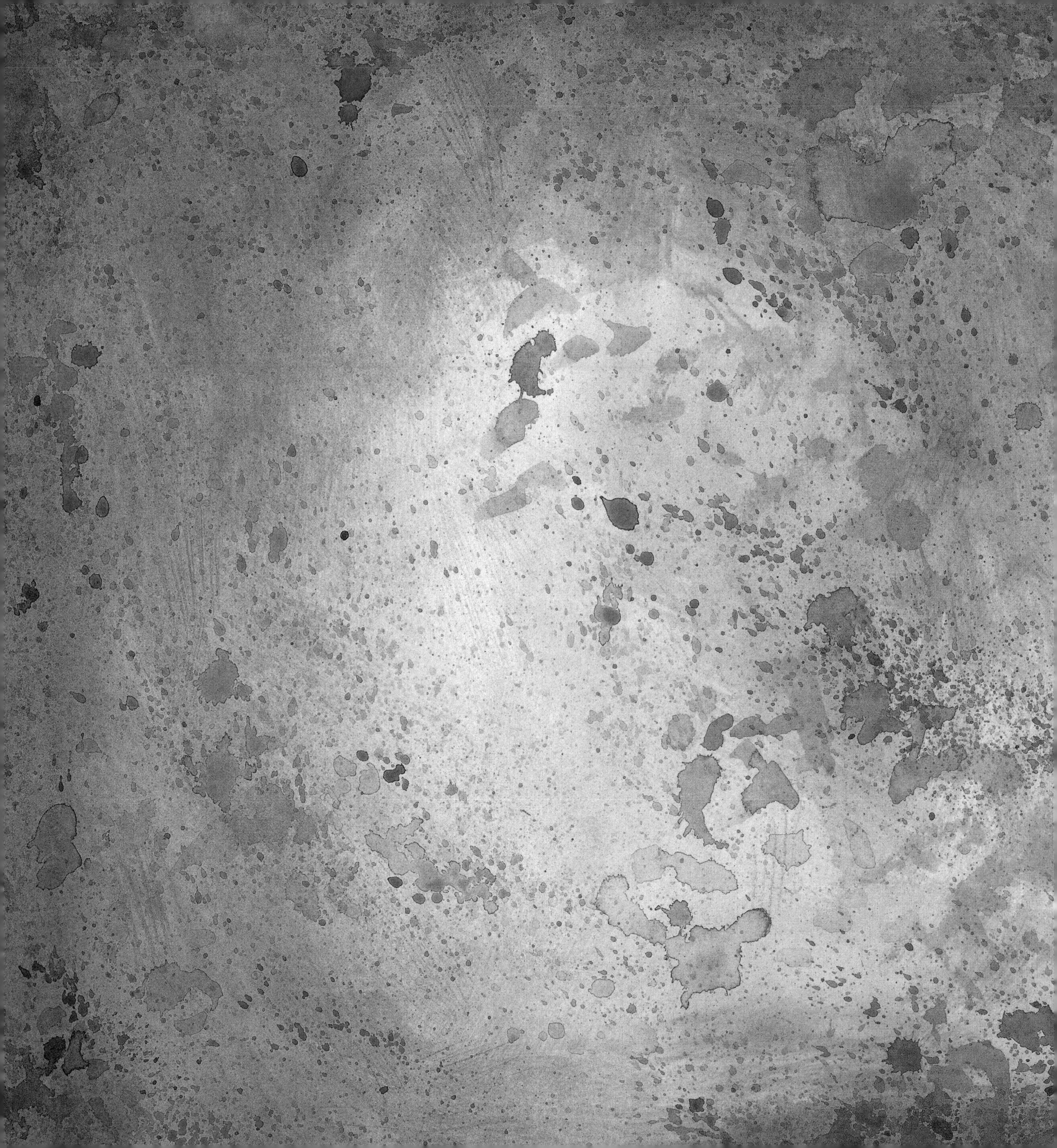